2014

D1135004

FAERIEGROUND

The Two Mothers

Book Seven

BY BETH BRACKEN AND KAY FRASER
ILLUSTRATED BY ODESSA SAWYER

STONE ARCH BOOKS
a capstone imprint

FAERIEGROUND IS PUBLISHED BY
STONE ARCH BOOKS
A CAPSTONE IMPRINT
1710 ROE CREST DRIVE
NORTH MANKATO, MINNESOTA 56003
WWW.CAPSTONEPUB.COM

LIBRARY OF CONGRESS CATALOGING-IN-
PUBLICATION DATA IS AVAILABLE ON THE
LIBRARY OF CONGRESS WEBSITE.

ISBN: 978-1-4342-4490-1 (LIBRARY BINDING)

SUMMARY: WITH DANGER SURROUNDING
THEM, SOLI AND LUCY MUST TRY TO
DISCOVER WHAT'S CAUSING LUCY'S ILLNESS.

BOOK DESIGN BY K. FRASER
ALL PHOTOS © SHUTTERSTOCK WITH THESE
EXCEPTIONS: AUTHOR PORTRAIT © K FRASER
AND ILLUSTRATOR PORTRAIT © ODESSA
SAWYER

PRINTED IN THE UNITED STATES OF AMERICA
IN STEVENS POINT, WISCONSIN.
032013
007227WZF13

"Hope is the thing with feathers—"

Emily Dickinson

For my parents, Tom and Susan Bracken, who taught me how to build a nest. —b
Dedicado a mi abuela Luisa Zorrilla, el angel que me enseño a volar. —k

The second girl wanted to save the first girl.

But was it going to be possible? Would the faeries let her go? And at what price?

After all, a wish is a wish, and *not all wishes are good.*

Chapter 1

Lucy

All I know is that Caro has taken me.

I was with the Ladybirds, I was sick—I still am

sick. I couldn't see. And then Caro took me

and then I was gone.

Someone is carrying me. I think we are flying.

The air is cold, and it feels good on my feverish

body.

"Where are we going?" I ask.

"Be quiet," Caro says. Her voice is different.

Meaner.

A shiver runs down my spine.

"We need to move faster," she says. "They'll soon be looking for her. Mikael, hurry up."

The arms around me tighten and we fly faster.

So it is not her arms I am in.

The sound of wings, flapping. The feel of wind.

Chapter 2

Soli

"This can't be happening," I whisper.

I pace back and forth in the small tent, my hands shaking from frustration. "Lucy was just here. How could you let her disappear?"

Motherbird doesn't reply.

She just stares at me, her cool eyes lingering on my face.

Kheelan grabs my hands. "Soli, we'll figure this out. We'll find her."

"They've taken her to the Crows, of course," Motherbird says.

"I thought Caro was a friend," Kheelan says. "I trusted her. Mostly."

Motherbird shoots us a sad smile. "Caro the Betrayer? A friend?" she says. "How did you think she received that name?"

"I thought she betrayed the queen," Kheelan says.

"She was given that name at birth," Motherbird says. "We gave it to her, because we saw what she would do."

I can't listen anymore. "Will she kill Lucy?" I ask.

Motherbird doesn't answer. "You will leave at sunrise to search for your friend," she tells me. "Your mother will show you the way."

"But Calandra is blind," Kheelan says.

Motherbird smiles at me. "She'll find her way there."

I think about my real mother. My mother at home.

She would be strong, tender, fair. She would want me to be fair and to fight.

"I don't trust her," I say. "Calandra."

"Your mother holds the key to finding the Crows," Motherbird says. "Without her, Lucy has no chance. And neither, young princess, do we."

"I wish you wouldn't call her my mother," I say. "I know she's my mother, but she isn't, not really."

Motherbird smiles. "I know," she says. "But

you're her only daughter. Her Hope."

Chapter 3

Lucy

I must have fallen asleep, because I wake up tangled in feathers.

My stomach drops. We seem to be falling.

"You're safe," the man whispers. His voice is low, almost a grunt.

And then we land. The man—Mikael—places me on my feet. The ground underneath me is reassuringly firm.

"Hurry up, Mikael. Could you be any slower?" Caro's voice is shrill.

I thought she was my friend, but I'm learning quickly that I never should have trusted her.

I try to remember if I told her anything important when we were locked in the cell together.

Anything I shouldn't have said.

Anything she could use against me, and against Soli.

"Where are we?" I ask.

"We are with the Crows," Caro says. "My people. Now be quiet."

Someone pokes me in the back, and I start walking—slowly, because it hurts. My whole body still aches, and I'm sweaty just from the effort of standing.

"Hurry up," Caro says. "They're waiting for us."

We walk, my hands bound behind me, Mikael behind me, Caro ahead of me, walking faster and faster.

"Remember that she's ill, Caro," Mikael says quietly.

"I don't care," Caro snaps. "My father is waiting."

Then I hear singing.

A sweet, soft lullaby. I am still blind, but images flash in my mind.

A lake. A castle.

The blue, blue sky, and a murder of crows.

I try to free my hands. I try to run.

The sound is beautiful, calling me toward it.

"Cover her ears right away," Caro says. "We need her alive, and the Sirens would swallow her."

My ears are muffled. The beautiful sound disappears and everything turns black.

Chapter 4

Soli

Calandra looks like an old woman.

Two days ago she looked almost as young as me. Now her hair has grayed. She can't be that old—I think she was young when she married my father, the king—but she looks old.

"Hope," she whispers. Her eyes are glazed. I think she must be blind.

"I need your help," I say, choosing my words carefully. "The Crows have taken Lucy."

"I told you Caro was not your friend," she says. A grin cracks her face. "Listen to your mother."

I clench my fists. "How do you feel?" I ask.

She shrugs, her unseeing eyes staring up at the roof of the tent. "I feel finished," she says.

"Motherbird says you can help me," I say. "That you can bring me to the Crows." And even as I say it, I worry. A dying woman is my only chance? My only hope?

"I can bring you there," she says. A frown flickers across her face and is gone, replaced with strength.

"Can you see anything?" I ask, bending closer.

"I don't need eyes to find that dark place,"
she says. She begins to sit up. "Are we leaving
now?"

"At dawn," I tell her. "Please be ready."

"I'll be ready," she says. "Tomorrow will be the
test—for all of us."

Chapter 4

Lucy

Someone gives me a warm drink, something in a wooden cup—a milky drink that's sweet with honey.

As I sip it, blurs take form in my eyes. The blurs become shapes—then light—then sight. Then a man like a bird stands in front of me.

I try not to panic, but he's terrifying. He reminds me of the man I saw in the Ladybird tent—an evil shape, a Crow.

But when he comes closer and takes my cup, I see that his eyes are soft. "You're the same age as my daughter," he says.

"I'm not your daughter, though, right?" I say. "You never know around here."

He laughs. "No. Her name is Violet. And she's at home with her mother. I am Mikael. I helped bring you here."

He is a Crow, then.

I don't know if I can trust anyone.

"Enough small talk," Caro says. I turn my head and see her, sitting cross-legged on the stone floor. She looks like she did in the cell we shared. Except that now she doesn't look like someone who could be my friend.

"Why did you bring me here, Caro?" I ask.

"My father needs you here," she says. "He is the head of the Crows. And that's all I'll tell you. For now."

But I sense arrogance in her words. She's proud to be this man's daughter. She'll tell me more, if I ask her right.

"I knew you were someone important," I say slowly. Caro straightens and a smile crosses her face. "I could tell from the second I met you."

"You were right, then," she says.

"And you knew so much," I say. "About the queen. About how she came to power. About Soli."

"I know more," she says. "I know so much about you. I know why you're really here, in the faerieground."

Now I'm surprised. "I thought we were here because Calandra wanted her daughter back," I say.

"No," she says. "That's just part of it."

Mikael coughs. It sounds like a warning. But Caro pays no attention.

"Don't you know anything, you stupid girl?" she says. "Don't you know who your mother is?"

I wait.

"Your mother is a witch," she says. "That's why we cast her out."

Chapter 5

Lucy

In the story Caro tells me,
there are two sisters.

One of the sisters was dark. The other was light.

Andria and Calandra.

They lived in Mearston, just outside Willow Forest. And one of them believed in faeries.

Calandra spent every day in the woods, trying to find faeries. She'd follow the smallest twinkle of light, the merest glimmer. Even as a little girl, she believed that she was meant to find her way to the faerieground.

And finally, one day, she did.

She plucked a four-leaf clover, caught a firefly, made a wish.

She was seventeen.

The first faerie she saw was the prince.

"And I think you can imagine how the rest of the story goes," Caro says.

So I ask about my mother.

Chapter 6

Soli

The sun begins to rise.

We walk through the cold woods. Kheelan leads the way, holding my hand. Jonn, Kheelan's father, helps Calandra down the path.

Kheelan moves as though the woods are his playground. His hand is rough, and warm, and safe.

"How are you?" he asks.

"I'm mostly tired," I say. "And worried about Lucy."

"I understand," he says. "I'm worried about her too."

A little bubble of jealousy grows inside me. Until he squeezes my hand.

We come to a fork in the path. "I don't know the way," he says. He looks back. Jonn and Calandra are far behind us. So he pulls me behind a tree and kisses me.

"Will we ever be real?" I ask, and he knows what I mean.

"I think so," he says. "Once this is over."

"What will it be like, once it's over?" I ask.

He shrugs. "I don't know," he says. "We should have asked the Ladybirds. I expect that they know."

It's comforting, thinking that those old faeries know what's to come.

I try to imagine myself a princess, a queen. But just a few days ago I was a kid at a school.

"Whatever happens—" Kheelan begins, but I cut him off.

"Whatever happens will happen," I say.

And then I kiss him again.

For a minute, I forget to be afraid.

And then Jonn and Calandra have caught up to us and we must keep on.

As we walk, Calandra says, "I want Soledad to help me."

Jonn catches my eye. "Is that all right with you?" he asks.

I nod, but I'm nervous. I take her arm anyway. Jonn and Kheelan walk a few steps ahead of us. Every so often, Kheelan glances back to smile at me.

"I think there are things you want to ask me," Calandra says softly.

She's right. "I don't know where to start," I admit.

"Begin with the beginning," she says. "And I'll do my best. We have a long walk."

"Why would the Crows take Lucy?" I ask. "If they want me, why not take me? Or you? She's a human girl. And she's sick."

"I was a human girl once," Calandra says.

She laughs. "That didn't stop them from using me to their advantage."

"Why you, then?" I ask.

"Being a sister," she says. "It came with a price."

We are quiet for a while. The woods are darkening, though I know it can't even be noon yet. Maybe, I think, we are getting nearer to the Crows.

Then I say, "I didn't know you had a sister."

"You know her well," Calandra says. "She still lives in the house where we grew up. Only now, I think, she stays out of the woods."

"Andria," I whisper. Of course.

So Kheelan was right.

"But you mustn't blame yourself, Soledad," she says.

And then I'm confused. "For what?" I ask.

"For breaking the spell that made us safe here," she says. "For the blindness. For Lucy being taken."

Jonn and Kheelan are beside us. They have heard everything.

"The spell was bound to her blood," Kheelan says. "And her blood is Lucy's blood."

"But it's mine, too," I say.

"Only half of it," Jonn says. "The rest of yours is faerie."

Chapter 6

Lucy

"I only know that she was left behind," Caro says.

My mother, she means.

"Calandra was forced to choose," Mikael adds. "Between the king, who she loved, and her sister, who she also loved."

"So she chose the king," I say. "Soli's father."

"And then we chose her," Caro says. The look of warning that Mikael shoots her is sharp, but she doesn't care. "We chose her," she goes on, "and we made her our spy."

Mikael sighs. "We can't say any more," he says.

Then there is a sharp rap at the door. Caro opens it, and a tall, strong man steps inside. He has long black hair and eyes like coals.

"Father," she says. "I have brought you the witch's daughter."

The man nods. "Thank you, Caro," he says. "You've done well."

Caro smiles. Her teeth glitter white.

Then the man steps forward and grabs my arm. "Come," he says.

Mikael grabs my other arm. The two men pull
me down a hallway.

This isn't like Calandra's palace. This building
is perfectly kept up. Every corner sparkles.
There are shiny objects on tiny shelves and
bright lamps that line the hallway.

They bring me to a room.

"We lost Calandra," Caro's father tells me.
"Now we need her sister."

My blood turns cold. "Why?" I ask.

"She asks a lot of questions," Mikael says.

"So I see," says Caro's father. Then he turns back to me. "We need the witch. You must make her come here."

I think of my mother at home. Knowing that I'm here, in the faerieground, knowing that I'm in a dangerous place. The place that took her sister.

Although maybe it wasn't so dangerous then.

"She won't come," I say.

"Not even to save her daughter?" Caro's father asks. "Doesn't she love you?"

Mikael frowns. "Easy, Georg," he mutters.

"Well, doesn't she?" Georg, Caro's father, asks again. "Wouldn't she risk everything for you? Don't you think she'd feel horrible if she knew you were here, dying, and you had decided to not let her save you?"

"I'm not dying," I whisper.

"Yes," Georg says. "You are."

Chapter 7

Soli

We have walked for hours.

Calandra is doing worse than before. Her body is so warm she gives off waves of heat. But her skin is dry. All the warmth just lives inside her. Killing her.

We walk. We take turns helping Calandra cross streams, step over rocks. Sometimes she can walk on her own. Other times she must be carried. Jonn does that, holds her body up. He treats her gently, like a queen. He arranges her skirt so that she is covered. He wipes dirt from her cheek.

When he catches me watching, he blushes.

And all the time, there are crows overhead, circling.

"What will we do once we arrive?" I ask Kheelan.

He frowns. "That will be up to you," he says.

But Motherbird didn't tell me what to do.

As if he's reading my mind, he says, "You'll know what to do."

"Calandra will have to help," I say.

But when I turn to look at her, Jonn has laid her body down on the path behind us.

"What's wrong?" I ask. Kheelan and I run back toward them.

"She can't go any farther," Jonn says. "She'll die."

"Can't you carry her?" Kheelan asks. Jonn shakes his head.

"Is it a curse? Maybe the Crows won't let her near them," I say.

Jonn shakes his head again. "I don't think so," he tells me. "I think she's dying. So you have a choice," he says, looking up at me. His look is even and kind. "She can die in my arms on the way to the Crows. Or she can die here, on our land, in your kingdom."

I sink to my knees next to my mother.

My not-real mother. My faerieground mother. The mother who birthed me.

"I need her help, though," I say. "I don't even know how to talk to the Crows."

"You will have to do that alone, I'm afraid," Jonn says. "No matter where she dies."

"Then she should die here," I say. "I don't want her to die on their land."

Jonn sighs. "She wouldn't want that either," he says. "For all of her faults, for all of her mistakes—she loved her kingdom."

My kingdom, now.

"Would you like to say goodbye?" I ask him.

A tear slips down Jonn's cheek, and he nods.

Kheelan looks surprised, but he takes my hand and we step away.

"I think they were in love," I say.

He shakes his head. "Impossible," he says.

We glance back. Jonn is on his knees. He raises Calandra's hand to his lips, kisses it, and rises. She says something we can't hear, and he nods. Then he walks away from her, and away from us.

"I'll wait here," Kheelan tells me.

I step closer to Calandra and kneel beside her. Her eyes are open, but I know she's still blind. "Soledad," she whispers, her voice dry and thick. "Soli."

I take a deep breath. "You can call me Hope," I say. "If you want to."

She smiles. "Thank you," she says. "But I know it isn't your true name."

She and I are quiet for a while.

Then she reaches up and strokes my cheek.

"Beware the Sirens," she says. "They'll try to stop you. Hold fast to Kheelan and Jonn, and the three of you can help each other through. Jonn knows the way. I told him the path."

"Okay," I say.

"And when you meet Georg, be careful," she says. "He is a liar and a cheat. He'll try to trick you," she says. "You can never trust a Crow. Their stories are always lies."

"How can I save Lucy?" I ask.

She sighs. "The same way I saved Andria," she tells me. "You must stay. And Lucy must leave. She isn't the one they want. Andria is. But they'll take you."

"Andria was in danger once?" I ask.

Calandra nods. "More than danger. She was entranced by the faerieground, by the Crows. She'd have done anything to stay here. She would have become one of them. And they wanted her."

Chapter 8

Lucy

They put me into a room.

I think it must be Caro's room. It feels like a

place where a girl my age would live. It smells

like her.

They leave me on a bed. It's the softest thing

I've laid on in days, ever since I first came to

the faerieground.

It's amazing that it was just a few days ago. I

kissed Jaleel at school and Soli saw me, and she

was angry, and we fought in the woods, and

she wished me away.

Now she's a princess and I'm dying.

Chapter 9

Soli

"Andria wanted to be a Crow?"
I ask, shocked.

Calandra tells me.

As a girl, Andria loved the woods. She spent every minute there. She talked about the faerieground all the time. She never bothered to make real friends, so enchanted was she with the idea of the faeries inside Willow Forest.

And then one day, she made a wish. She found herself in the faerieground, and the first person she saw was a Crow.

The Crows had a plan.

They wanted to kill the Willow King, but they didn't know how. When they had Andria, they realized their weapon.

They would make him fall in love with the human girl and then she would kill him. And in exchange, they would make her appear as a faerie.

"They didn't know she had a sister," Calandra tells me. "They didn't know I would follow her, and fight for her."

"What did you do?" I ask.

She shrugs. "I took her place."

"So you did trick my father," I say. "And you did kill him."

Her blind eyes close. "No," she whispers.

She tells me more. Once she had convinced them to let her stay in Andria's place, the Crows sent her to the Willow Kingdom. They used a glamour to make her look like a faerie and cast their spell. If anyone found out she was human, and removed the spell, she would become sick and die.

She found the king and she told him the Crows' plan. She assumed he would remove the glamour and send her home.

But he couldn't.

He tried. They spent days, weeks, months together. But the Crows' spell was difficult and he couldn't do it.

Instead, quite by accident, they fell in love.

They were married and happy and a baby was born. They named her Hope.

And then the king became ill, and he died.

As Calandra mourned, the kingdom fell into
disrepair. Her people turned on Calandra.
They knew she had been with the Crows. They
did not know she was human. They thought
she was a Crow, sent to kill the king and
destroy the kingdom.

The Ladybirds came in the night and took the
baby away. And after that, Calandra was at
war with everyone. Only her guards were her
friends. She spent the next years waiting for
someone to make a wish in the woods.

She finishes the tale. Then she takes my hand.

"I dreamed of seeing you again," she says. "I thought I never would."

"I'm sorry," I say. "I hope you know I was safe and loved."

"Yes, I know," she says. "You are strong and beautiful and brave. My precious girl. My Hope. Remember to always turn the stones."

Then she takes a deep breath, squeezes my hand, and is gone.

Chapter 10

Soli

We keep walking through the woods,
her body left behind.

I don't like leaving it. It seems cruel and unfair.
But Jonn says someone will be sent for it, and
she will be buried as a queen.

Kheelan takes my hand. He and Jonn and I
walk, silent, through the forest. We come to a
small, gnarled plum tree, dripping with fruit,
and we stop.

"The Sirens are beyond this tree," Jonn says.
"You mustn't listen to them." Kheelan and I
nod. Then I grab Jonn's hand. We all squeeze
hands, take deep breaths, and run.

Beth & Kay

Kay Fraser and *Beth Bracken* are a designer-editor team in Minnesota.

Kay is from Buenos Aires. She left home at eighteen and moved to North Dakota—basically the exact opposite of Argentina. These days, she designs books, writes, makes tea for her husband, and drives her daughters to their dance lessons.

Beth and her husband live in a light-filled house with their son, Sam. She spends her time editing, reading, daydreaming, and rearranging her furniture.

Kay and Beth both love dark chocolate, Buffy, and tea.

Odessa

Odessa Sawyer is an illustrator from Santa Fe, New Mexico. She works mainly in digital mixed media, utilizing digital painting, photography, and traditional pen and ink.

Odessa's work has graced the book covers of many top publishing houses, and she has also done work for various film and television projects, posters, and album covers.

Highly influenced by fantasy, fairy tales, fashion, and classic horror, Odessa's work celebrates a whimsical, dreamy and vibrant quality.